MY OLD FRIEND
SILENCE

MY OLD FRIEND
SILENCE

COLLECTION OF SHORT STORIES

Sonya Khorshidi

Translator
Fatemeh Namdarian

PARTRIDGE
A Penguin Random House Company

ISBN: Softcover   978-1-4828-3031-6
               eBook   978-1-4828-3032-3

Print information available on the last page.

To order additional copies of this book, contact
Toll Free 800 101 2657 (Singapore)
Toll Free 1 800 81 7340 (Malaysia)
orders.singapore@partridgepublishing.com

www.partridgepublishing.com/singapore

CONTENTS

ABOUT THE AUTHOR

Sonya was born in 1989 in Tehran. She has a degree in Bachelor of Arts. Currently she is a freelance Search Marketing Analyst Based in Kuala Lumpur, Malaysia. She found her passion in writing when she was 15 years old and since then she dreamed of writing stories and creating characters in her mind. Finally she found her courage to put pen on paper and write her first book, the collection of short stories, *My Old Friend Silence*.

For Farah and Coco

PREFACE

This might be related to some individual's character that they engage with their environment through internal dialogues. After a while, this enables them to comprehend their surroundings, their meanings and concepts.

I always found connecting with surroundings and thinking about their forms attractive and entertaining. In most parts of my stories, they play the roles of my characters and transfer their feelings. It is fascinating that how people, these magnificent beings, with their behaviors and moves inspire me to write and create characters who encounter unexpected unordinary events.

These stories are a part of people's hidden but attractive lives. This book is my understanding of people's interactions with others and the quality of their relationships with them as well as their private lives and reactions towards their emotional issues.

"Cold Like Silence"

Rare moments are always accompanied by silence; like silence in the interval of a melody before it rises to the crescendo. When breaths are held, eyes are closed, then it races towards the peak and hearts start galloping.

In that silence, everyone becomes no one, even the musicians. It's a moment when everything is motionless. That moment is the hardest, when the silence ends, and it reaches its peak. It's when we ask ourselves who we are. What are we doing here? What do we want from life? Do we want to carry on living like this? We ask again, 'Who are we?'

I burst into laughter looking at the movements of my hand; my wrist that moves the knife along with the rhythm. I think, 'It's amazing that when I'm doing the simplest most basic and trivial things in the world, such deep thoughts cross my mind.'

I ask myself, 'How many oranges have I peeled in my life? Maybe over a hundred? Maybe more, or less, it doesn't really matter.'

The smell, the sticky, cool feeling of oranges always reminds me of summer school holiday when I used to sit cross-legged in the middle of the living room peeling an orange, trying not to cut the fruit inside and hoping for it to be seedless. Then I would stuff my mouth with orange segments, one after another so that I nearly choked. I would also watch out for my mom not to see me in that state, as she would always say, "Small bites, small! Easy kid, easy!"

It has been a while since those hot, humid, noisy days. I am now in a place far from my childhood home, in an area where it's cold and filled with silence almost throughout the year.

I don't know what it is about the cold that carries this silence. That might be because everywhere is bare and bareness comes with silence.

I separate the orange segments hoping that they will be seedless. I put them in my mouth voraciously. The juice is dripping from my lips and I think to myself, 'No, exported oranges which are piled on top of each other in silos for months don't have the same flavor as the old ones.' But the smell is the same. The fact about a familiar smell is that in less than a second, every single cell of your body reviews the memories that smell reminds you of. I think this happens very swiftly. But the brain cannot remember and follow all those memories at once. And that's why when we smell a remembered fragrance, we get confused, really confused. We may recollect one or two memories, but not more than that. In this moment (or at this moment), I prefer not to remember anything from the past.

My memories make me feel like an ignoble prince whose tomorrow is unknown to him; whether he'll sit on the throne or be sent into exile forever.

I aimlessly cut the orange peel into cubes. I am conscious of the silence around me. Every now and then I hear the sound of the logs sparking in the fireplace, and nothing else.

I look through the window. The snow has become heavier and the sky light pink, feminine now. I walk towards the window. I look at the frozen lake which is covered with several layers of snow.

The trees with their desiccated branches surround the lake as if they intend to preserve it. Perhaps we should understand silence in order to be able to feel the spirit of winter, or maybe silence is the language of cold or …. I don't know … I only know that cold is pretty and silence the prettiest.

"Mirror"

No one expects things to be this way, when they reach this stage of their lives. Now the only thing he wishes is for this storm to be over and he prays for God to take him to the other side. He always believed that whatever happened he could accept and tolerate, but maybe he was wrong, like many other mistakes he had made.

He looked at himself at the mirror and with his shaking hands, smoothed the wrinkles at either side of his mouth. It didn't seem to make a difference, but to make sure he decided to put on his spectacles to see his face more clearly. It made him happy when he remembered where he had placed them. They were on the arms of the sofa.

He picked them up briskly, more briskly than he had moved around the last three weeks and put them on, walked towards the mirror and tried to stretch his skin with his fingers in different directions. A faint smile appeared on his lips, as he was bending and his nose touched the mirror.

He wasn't the only one who missed his wrinkle-free face. The mirror was also not accustomed to any other faces except the old man's and his tired, young grandchild who would visit him occasionally.

He looked at the fine woodwork around the mirror and with the same fingers, which were stretching his face; he touched the solid, red wood. His wrinkles moved back to their original shape. He moved his hand around the finely-carved flowers and touched all the petals. He was cautious not to jostle the mirror. It had been awhile since it had been fixed loosely to the wall, with a nail.

Whenever he looked at himself in the mirror, he counted the carved flowers. This counted them this time as well. Eight! He thought to himself 'How come this mirror and these flowers have remained intact and beautiful, but I have grown so old and got so many deep wrinkles.' Once he was a dignified and handsome man. As dignified as the mirror, today and tomorrow.

He was cold and bored. He had taken all his pills after breakfast and checked his face in the mirror. He had contacted his only grandchild and listened to his recorded message as usual. He hated this machine. Each time he heard the message, he would curse it and cut off the phone.

He had flattened the bed sheets three times already but the right corner of the top sheet was creased. Slowly he walked towards his bed and smoothed it out. He stepped back to ensure it looked neat. He sat on the only chair in the kitchen and waited for the telephone to ring. To not become tired, he leaned his chin on his arms.

As he was going to the window, he suddenly heard something which made him curious; a loud bang. He changed his direction and went to the door. Opened it. He shivered, it was cold. There were some youths with flashy orange outfits in the snow. He counted them and murmured: 'Four'.

These days shoveling the snow is such a hassle; it's noisier and causes a lot of transport glitches. The neighboring men used to step out of their houses at certain time of the day carrying their snow shovels on their shoulders. They would clean the frozen snow off the pavements and in front of their homes. The children would throw snowballs at each other among their fathers' dancing shovels. Women would entertain their families with warm food later in the evening.

He could still hear the wooden shovels being dragged on the frozen ground and people's steps in the hollow snow reminding him of happy kids and their glowing cheeks. The cold filled his whole body. The past is gone. He took a deep breath. His lungs were filled with cold. He turned around and closed the heavy wooden door behind him.

...

He was about to fall asleep, but the silence was broken by the noise of a smashed glass. He jumped out of bed. He was still shivering with cold; he put on his old, checked robe. His toe hit the table next to the bed. He groped for the switch and turned it on. There was no mirror on the wall anymore.

He gently closed his eyes. He didn't even want to see the broken mirror on the floor. It would only make him gloomier. He put on his plastic slippers to protect his feet from the small pieces of mirror. He turned off the light. The room became dark. A cold wind blew inside from the cracks in the door and walls. He pulled the woolen blanket up to his chin. Took a deep breath and gently closed his eyes and went to a place beyond his awareness. Suddenly he felt better; he was there, one step closer to eternity.

"Coco"

The little girl was walking rapidly on her small feet. The wind was blowing her corduroy coat around her bare legs. Suddenly, she noticed how fast she was walking, so she slowed down. It took her a while to catch her breath, though. She took a deep breath and as her fourth grade teacher had taught her, tried to calm herself down thinking, "Calm down, everything's going to be alright! None will know."

She pressed her straw bag to her chest and took fast steps. She was out of breath, her nose was cold and her narrowed eyes were looking ahead with hope and determination mixed with fear and worry; as if she had the biggest aim in the whole world.

With her little hands, she turned her bag around and squeezed it more tightly. She was not listening to her brain anymore; whatever was in her bag was making her decide what to do next. She could hear her heart beats as well as another little heart which would fill each interval between her own. What was this feeling? Was she experiencing love?

For the first time, she looked back. It seemed like everyone was busy with their life. No one was paying any attention to her, not even a quick glance.

She saw a cute boy her age or maybe a bit older. She walked faster to attract his attention to her bare knees. But when she got closer to the boy, he was gone. Suddenly, she felt sad. She thought: "Does anyone love me? Does anyone see me at all? Does anyone know what I have done wrong?"

Her little bag moved and she came back to the present. She started walking hopefully. She had stolen something, alive, a beating heart, a warm body which could breathe in and out. She didn't know if it belonged to anyone or not. She only knew that she was holding that little creature in her straw wrapped tightly with a red ribbon knowing that no one can trust these ribbons.

She had begged her mom to buy her the bag. She wanted to take it with her to grandma's last spring. Now after a few months, she had hidden something in it without permission.

She was tired. She stopped at a corner and loosened the ribbon. Frist, she saw dark shadows of crystal balls which turned into two beautiful green eyes when they were touched by sunlight. They were looking at her with a dozen questions.

She forgot everything as she was captivated by those eyes. She breathed a sigh of relief. She had to choose a name for it. She always liked names starting with 'C'. Pressing the bag against her heart joyfully, she stood up and whispered: "Coco."

"Butter and Carrot Cake"

People say loneliness is the greatest poverty and the last thing anyone should wish for. But artists are always lonely. Being alone is what they need, what makes their lives more beautiful and gives them the ability to create.

Sometimes I go to the small balcony of my room and I look at the traffic, the small heads and shoulders inside their iron boxes. They remind me of my brother's old, red toys which we used to play with on the edge of the carpet in our kitchen. The fluff on the carpet would stop our toys and throw them off the track.

My car, sometimes, would be parked for a while on the carpet as I was busy pushing crumbs into the wool threads.

I was also lonely as a kid. However, it didn't mean anything to me. Reviewing childhood memories is something odd and being a grownup means having troubles, utility bills and dealing with your boss and colleagues…but nothing is worse than a nosy neighbor.

I don't dare open the blind in the living room as I'm afraid she might peep in. Sometimes I forget to close the blind in the kitchen after cleaning the window. I can see her looking furtively through the window of her little kitchen. She pretends she is busy doing the washing up, but after a while she forgets that she was acting, her foamy hands stop moving. That is my favorite moment as I can catch her out by looking straight into her eyes. I smile or wave at her. Normally she freaks out. God knows how many glasses or dishes she has cracked or broken.

Ms. Sal makes me cakes every now and then. The other night she made some carrot cake. The smell of butter was stronger than carrots on the staircase. She never uses the doorbell, but always bangs on my old, wooden door with the back of her hand.

Early on when I moved to this neighborhood, I didn't know anyone. Of course now, except Ms. Sal, I don't know many more. She has asked me several times why no one visits me, if my parents are alive or if I have a boyfriend. After she is done with her questions, she puts on a sympathetic mask and says: 'You know, I'm old and I may die soon. Who will visit you when I'm gone?' And then she starts asking more questions about my past, present and future. I wonder why an old woman who has been married three times with several grandchildren and great grandchildren, who never visit her, should be worried about me and my loneliness. She is alone herself. She has me and I have her.

My only excuse to say goodbye to her is that I have a performance tomorrow and I have to practice. I say this while I have a notebook or a bow in my hand and because it works. She looks at her old flowery slippers, the fabric stained with brown coffee and says: 'You artists work from morning to night and at the end of the day, you get peanuts.'

She is right, though. She says this while she is leaving my house, without looking at me. She adds: 'I am taking my sleeping pills at 8.30 and will be in bed by 9.00.' She is making it clear that I am allowed to practice only till then.

Sometimes I miss her when she leaves and I think to myself: 'Seriously, if one day Ms. Sal is gone, there will be no one but me, my instrument, a cat, a worn-out car and piles of takeaway boxes in the kitchen cabinet smelling of butter.'

"Fate and Destiny"

The alleys in this district were full of hippie cafés which looked more like warehouses, with seven or eight broken tables and chairs in the middle of them. The floors would be bare cement and the ceilings wrapped with yellow, red, green and grey cables.

With empty boxes, the bricks left over from construction and thick books, they would make a so-called bar and kitchen as small as a match box, which would break the whole space into two. The owners would not make any effort to arrange the furniture harmoniously.

In the first few weeks after I moved to this area, this café became an inseparable part of my life. I would spend a few hours in one of these cafés. Sometimes I would look at the walls, ceiling, floor and specially the chairs and tables while I was drinking my coffee, which was cold from the moment it was brought from the kitchen.

I would picture Lily who used go down the winding roads and alleys and knock on everyone's door to buy their decorative furniture and items. She would always offer 20 bucks for everything. 20 was her favorite number and it was her starting price.

Whenever I purchased something, and asked her to guess how much I had spent on it, she would say: "20!" It didn't matter if it was a genuine leather belt or a plastic hair clip.

Lily was someone who would buy the thickest and most expensive books whenever we went to a bookstore. She believed those books would change her life. In reply to the inquiring look in my eyes, she would act as if she was the president's spokesman trying to cover up his affair in front of dozens of microphones and journalists. Then she would say: "I will read this one to the end. It is worth it!"

But I knew that only 5 or 10 pages of the book would be read. Then I would see the book covered with dust next to our bed. That would be the time when the book would be transferred to a small, and beautiful bookshelf, which had turned into storage for Lily's new, unfinished books.

Lily was the simplest and bravest person I had ever met and I loved her. I always preferred to love someone than to be in love with them, because love is like a dark and narrow road between tall, thick walls. I was never the kind to fall in love, as life without love is hard and complicated enough. I have learnt to choose the quickest and simplest way to reach my goals, because moments arrive like a shooting star from a distance, and pass by rapidly and then burn out.

Youth is when you have to enjoy your solitude and freedom. But when time passes and you get used to a routine, you will realize that life is like a nest that you cannot make on your own. That's how I see it, anyway.

Amongst all those cafés, in those old, narrow, humid alleys, one of them has become my destiny. I love its disharmony, untidiness and dissonance. I love the coffee that is always cold, and the memories of Lily and I who used to come here become alive, and when I leave this place they run away from me.

"Mondays and Wednesdays"

Bismarck was one of the two battleships made by the German Navy before the Second World War. Named after the first chancellor, it came to the same end as the rest. It sank in June 1941 in the South Atlantic Ocean, after two years of continuous active duty.

The old man with the checked beige-brown, fury hat which I think was a 60s design raised his right eyebrow. Scratching his big, eagle-shaped nose, he said, "It was not the South Atlantic Ocean, my son! It was the North Atlantic Ocean." The other old group members nodded and agreed. Another old man wearing a red tie with a geometric navy blue pattern continued: "Europe is closer to the North Atlantic Ocean."

A few moments later, an elderly man in a dark brown corduroy vest waved his hand in the air and said: "I believe it was all the British fault… these British people! But Germany deserved it." And before he finished, the man with the red tie interrupted him: "Jack, I always thought you supported the social-democrat party."

Jack stopped grumbling and said: "What I was saying doesn't have to anything with that. Once I was a social democrat, but I didn't know the difference between Marxism and socialism. I was in my 20s, young and stupid. I was only a follower."

Everyone started nodding again and repeated: "Yes, we were young and stupid. We were only followers."

Then the women who have not given any opinions, started to talk about the cakes at the bakery in the 10th Avenue, and how they could get there with their kids by taking the 734, 736, or 376 buses. None of them knew the exact bus number. When the bus number had been forgotten, they discussed which cookies were the best. Sally always liked fresh cookies. At the end all of them agreed with her that coconut cookies were the best because they are whiter and less sweet.

...

Last week, my friends asked me which days of the week I hated the most, I replied without thinking: "Mondays and Wednesdays." Today was one of those days.

When I was a kid, my mum used to work in a car show room. She was the only female dealer there and her sales were always lower than the salesmen. Therefore, she would be threatened in the end year review meeting.

In her first year, one night when she came home I asked her to help me with my poor project work. But she replied: "No, honey! Not now! My head is exploding." Her reply was so strange to me that I couldn't sleep till morning worrying maybe my brain would explode as well, and what if it actually happened.

Today, at this moment I can understand what my mum felt like. I looked at my watch. The bus would arrive in half an hour to take the ladies and gentlemen back. I waited a bit for them to finish their conversation, but it seemed like an endless discussion. I announced the time with a smile and apology and we all walked towards the café.

I eyed the people and counted them. One was missing. I returned. Jack was standing in front of the battleship pictures. He took off his hat and held it in front of himself. I walked to him and called him: "Jack?"

He was still staring at the ships. "It's weird." he replied.

"What's weird?" I asked?

"Life!" he replied. He kept silence for a moment and then continued: "The fact that you are once at the peak of power, go to war and when you are old and wrecked, you sink in a deep ocean. Somewhere dark! Become a house for creatures in the deep ocean who you even do not know."

He took a deep breath. Put his hat on and remarked: "The life of a ship is like the life of a human being. At the end, there is only some memories and murmurs left of you."

"Dream # 2"

He blinked, and yawned. Stretching his soft, smooth body, he sat down and looked into my eyes steadily! The two green, glassy eyes I had known for years reflected his kind, tired, angry and naughty sprit. How could they flash all those mixed feelings at the same time? Although I reviewed this question like a mantra in my tired brain, I hadn't had an answer for it yet.

I was sitting on a velvet, cerise sofa, with my hands fisted, without moving. I felt like I was part of it, as If I had been sitting there for a long while.

It felt like I was chasing my childhood dreams: On a sunny day I was writing my dreams with my tiny pencil. My pencil was covered with many dancing silver stars and now after being sharpened again and again, there were only three stars left complete, one star with two points and another one with one point. The rest of them were dead and quiet. They had all been moved to a green bin bag, which was the mass grave for unusable stuff. Sometimes I would collect the shreds of the pencils in my fortune, plastic egg-shaped toy and when everyone was asleep, I would sneak out to the yard, dig a small hole and plant them in the hope that one day a star tree would grow.

I used to take care of that mysterious part of the yard for a long time. I was extremely careful not to let my godfather's giant, ugly dog go anywhere near it. When I grew up I learnt that star trees don't exist. I even don't want to remember those days anymore, they remind me how childish and stupid I was.

My pencil was shorter now. We were getting close to the New Year and the list of my wishes was getting shorter and shorter year by year. At the beginning of each line, I used to write the number of my wish and then the wish next to it; 1., 2., 3., 4., ... and today when I look at those lists I see that none of my dreams have come true except one. Maybe my dreams and my life were always more beautiful and exciting than the reality. Or maybe, I never had the courage to make them come true.

I forgot my past and my childhood when a warm, silky body touched me. It was getting bright. The snow had frozen behind the living room window. I was still reclining on the sofa. I moved my stiff body, bent and held the only dream of my life that had come true. I breathed him in with the whole capacity of my lungs. I stared at him. The eyes of my dream number 2 were full of dancing silver stars.

"DAYDREAMING"

Nothing is worse than noise pollution. The never-ending friction of wheels against the hot summer asphalt, horns blowing, and sellers by the road shouting: 'Buy, buy! Original Rolex, the latest model with a leather strap,...'

I wonder to myself whether there are any Rolex with leather straps. I have seen Rolex with metal straps only. As far as I remember my father's entire family, men and women, used to wear gold or silver ones, with or without diamonds, around their wrists. I think after the 80s, wearing a Rolex was not an advantage anymore; it was just an inseparable part of their life.

Before our separation, my brothers and I used to visit my cold and formal father's family once a year, during the New Year. But my mother would never accompany us. She would always have an excuse to free herself from these visits. She either had a cold, had got her period, or had a deadline.

My grandparent's house smelled of wood, walnut wood. Even the delicate ornamentation around the ceiling was carved out of wood. I always thought it needed millions of termites to eat it all up.

The huge fireplace in my grandfather's favorite place, library, spread a nostalgic feeling in the room. I always thought there was a hidden door behind the shelves which would lead to Dracula's house. Or under the red silk carpet in front of the fireplace, there might be a box of documents from the Second World War or from Nazis, or perhaps behind the Bouguereaus's oil painting, there was a chest full of gold bars.

I am not sure about my brothers, but I always made up many weird stories about that room. The room did not smell of walnut wood only, it was mixed up with my grandfathers' tobacco. Even the upholstery smelled of that familiar scent.

. . . .

The taxi driver started his third cigarette, inhaled it deeply and leaned his head against the seat. I tried to look dissatisfied and to attract his attention, I faked a cough. I moved in my seat several times and looked at him in the front mirror. But he didn't pay any attention. He took a small brush out of the left pocket of his uniform and started dusting the Buddha statue on his dashboard.

I wish I had a brush seven or eight times bigger than that I could remove my cat's fur from my trousers and T-shirts.

I tried to forget the awful state of my wardrobe, look through the window and pay attention to the traffic and people. It's a weird place. I thought to myself, 'How many people are happy on the other side of this window? How many of them really love someone wholeheartedly? Do they ever feel alone?'

Thinking was enough. My brain did not want to think about these issues. It wanted to indulge itself to somewhere safe, warm, and full of good feelings. Past? No! Future? Never! No time!

I run like I haven't run for ages, thirsty, full of joy. I run on the hot white, beach. The wind combs my hair. I run so fast that I lose control and I trip on the soft sands. Then I roll on the sand innocently. I lie on my back and with both hands open; I steal a fistful of sand. I let the sands run gently through my fingers and watch them as they sift gently till there are none left.

I sit facing the ocean cross-legged while the waves hit my body. With each wave, water washes the sands below me away. I look at what's happening childishly. I'm alone. But, no, my brain likes it when the people around me are happy.

A young couple are hugging each other so lovingly and with each wave they let out a scream out of excitement.

A father is making a sand castle with his children and the mother is kissing her husbands' head from behind rubbing sunblock on his shoulders. I enjoy the love, integrity, and nature.

All of a sudden, I crave for joining the ocean. I run towards it and I go with the first wave.

…

'Madam? Excuse me madam? Is this the place?'

I open my heavy eyelids. The taxi has stopped. I look through the window. The marble-faced apartment, number 94.

'Yes, this is my house. How much is it?'

'Mam? You paid me at the airport. Don't you remember?' says the taxi driver.

Without saying a word I pick up my little case. While I'm getting out of the taxi, I turn around and look at where I was sitting to see if I have left anything behind. There is nothing, but some grains of sand.

"American Cat"

Cold seasons, we all gather together around the warm chimney of a house made of bricks, crouch and stare into space or at the thick smoke of the chimney vanishing in the sky. None of us knows when this damn cold is getting over.

Years ago when I was newly-born, I kept asking the rest when the cold was going to be over. Nobody knew. So these days I just keep waiting.

There are, however, always some signs of when this cold season is giving way to a warm one and one is our neighbor's daughter. When she stops wearing her tasseled hat and over-sized pink wool gloves, then I can tell that the cold is gradually coming to an end.

Sometimes my grumbling stomach or someone who leans on me wakes me up. The only thing that helps me fall sleep again is remembering the smell of turkey on Thanksgiving Day around the neighborhood. We all become thankful, knowing that we will receive some good portions as well.

I go back to sleep thinking about this beautiful dream. But sometimes I can't. Walking quietly and carefully not to wake anyone, I go to the attic and then to the balcony of a big bedroom. Then to the yard which is now covered with twigs instead of fresh green grass.

The good thing about warm weather is that you can walk on fresh grass. I love the smell of it. Every now and then, when there is no one in the backyard I roll around on the grass while a little girl watches me through her bedroom window with admiration. I roll and roll until she starts smiling, then I look away. She stands there for a while and then walks away.

The sky is dark and cloudy. You even cannot see the moon and the stars. Nothing looks good in this season. No birds fly, or squirrels skip from one side of the road to another and disappear in the bushes, nor kids play. Nothing happens in this cold-icy season; everything is frozen.

I feel sleepy now, but I don't feel like going back to the roof where the others are. I walk up the stairs in front of the house feeling the warmth from underneath the door. I stick to the door and crouch. I close my eyes slowly and hibernate while thinking about Thanksgiving Day.

"Kind Bear"

S he rubbed her little, swollen hands together. Rubbed her fingers of one hand with the other and pinched between her fingers quickly and carefully. Then she bent slowly to take the glass oil container from the old, short stool next to her. It was smeared with many finger prints.

The container slipped, but she caught it at the bottom with her other hand. Her heart was in her mouth. For a moment she imagined the noise of breaking glass amid the 'Chakra Balancing' music and the effect on the prone naked body experiencing at the expense of hundreds of dollars worth of serenity. The scene seemed more disastrous than a nuclear bomb explosion or a Richter 7 earthquake. God knows how many glasses, vases, plates and fragile items slip from people's hands and break, but breaking things in this place was forbidden.

Yesterday Isabel called her to the office and asked her to smile more. Then she had corrected herself and repeated: 'Smile all the time. Serious, lifeless faces don't have a place in this business.'

If she were executive manager of a company, a pianist or a brain surgeon nobody would have expected her to smile 24/7. But she had thousands of thoughts on her mind. After so many years of experience she knew how to re-focus. She looked at the black mole on the man's left shoulder, stared at it for a moment, narrowed her eyes, took a deep breath, 'Are you ready, sir?' asked him with a soft voice.

'Yes' the man answered with a low voice and then nodded. She picked the oil carefully and poured it on the man's naked back. The less oil in the bottle, the more the smell odour of lavender spread around the room. She loved lavender; it would give her a sense serenity to mix with her fear. She massaged the man's neck, shoulders, back and top of his bottom repeatedly, clock- and anti-clock wise. Now it was the spine's turn. It was near his dorsal vertebra that the man groaned and lifted his face from the bed. 'Please, use less pressure! Go easy around that area.' he said. Then he put his back on the bed again and added: 'That part is very painful'. The smile faded from her face and she replied: 'Yes, sir! How is it now?'. Pressing his back less strongly. The man replied: 'Yes, yes, it is much better now. Thank you. Last week, I played golf an hour longer than usual and it has been painful ever since. I can't believe that playing for an extra hour would make my back hurt. I think I am getting old.'

The man laughed and then kept silent. She wanted to sympathies and talk with him, but the rules would not allow her to confide with costumers. She was supposed to smile and carry on working.

She had forgotten to smile while she was paying attention to her moving hands. With each pressure she could feel a shooting pain from her bones to the muscles of her shoulders. Then it would move to her arms, elbows, wrists and fingers.

She agreed with the man. Growing old happens gradually, in darkness and silence. Silence with pain, and pain in various forms and shapes. A pain like a wasp sting or burning, or a pain that you cannot ignore any more because it makes the world around you disappear.

Her pain was one of those pains. What she needed was time; 60 minutes of rest without naked bodies and the scent of lavender. She murmured in the ear of the man who was now snoring: 'Sir, it's over now...Sir?'

He moved and lifted his head off the bed, his saliva had dripped on the sheet. He looked at the old lady with his puffy eyes. She tried not to smile while she asked: 'Would you like some water or hot herbal tea?'

...

She closed the door gently. Walking slowly in the hall, she tried to avoid making eye contact with people.

She was still faking a smile. Without taking off her uniform, she opened the heavy wooden door and stepped out.

She stood still for a moment. The smell of freshly-mowed grass in the front courtyard was mixed with car exhausts. She had been missing the car horns and people noise in the streets. She walked towards the main road. She was so tired that if she hadn't controlled herself; she would have fallen. She was pulling herself forward, heading to the café on the corner of the road. She could see the red and yellow chairs on the sidewalk. The remaining 200 meters seemed as long as several kilometers.

She had arrived now. She sat on the red chair. A minute later a young girl put a menu in front of her and stood there with a smile that most probably her boss had asked her to fake, holding and a pen and piece of paper to take her order.

The old woman looked at the long menu. She didn't know what she wanted. The girl noticed her confusion and suggested 'Would you like a hot drink? You look tired.'

That was her life's best offer. She smiled at the girl and leaned back on the chair. Her whole body felt numb. She closed her eyes. Her nose was filled with the smell of lavender. She opened her eyes at the noise of a touch on the table. There was now a purple glass in front of her. She bent forward and stared at it. She smiled all across her face.

Sometimes, happiness comes from the most unpredictable places. She picked and took a sip of the coffee from the smiley kind bear cup.

"JAZZ AND LOVE"

She had forgotten that reality is different from words used to describe it. She had been living with her own words. Sometimes she couldn't see, hear, or touch anything. Words were only words only, but music was everything to her.

The music on the stage shook every cell in her body with joy. She couldn't tell whether it was the music, the place or both. One piece of music would start and end after another. She couldn't feel the moments passing by, as if her body had become resistant to change. Her nails and hair had stopped growing and she had stopped aging. She was just breathing, enjoying the music and waiting for her favorite tune.

The whole space was dark. There was only a dim light on the musicians, shining like a rare gem on the stage. Little lights wrapped around the Christmas tree with its red and golden ornaments reminded her of childhood memories where all the characters of stories were happy, dancing and singing. The dim lights were making the atmosphere more suitable for kids.

But with all that beauty, light and happiness something was wrong, or unbelievable. It was quite impossible to see all people of the city happy and dancing like the people at the table near her.

There was a couple who were sitting at the next table and weren't even having an eye contact with each other, never mind exchanging words. They were staring at the stage searching their world in amazement. They looked so relaxed.

...

To create that tune and its name was her decision. There is something obvious about decisions; they might be wrong. Because nobody is perfect and she knew that well.

The first time she heard that tune, only the two of them were together and she didn't feel anything. Now that it was performed in front of a crowd, she was proud. Somebody had written a song for her and it was supposed to be played for different audiences in many cafés and restaurants for years to come, from east to west. For people who had different histories. People who have been in love, or someone has been in love with them. Thinking about all these things would excite her.

"Life is the most unpredictable thing in this world", she thinks. She is sitting in a cosy corner of a café around a three-seat table and waiting for her tune.

She thought: "Waiting sometimes can kill you." The lead musician looked at her in the interval between two melodies, smiled and brought his instrument closer to his lips to play the next piece and made the atmosphere even more mysterious. She felt like she was the most special person there, as if she had travelled from the past to future.

She took a deep breath, rested her right leg on the left and pushed away the crumbled tissues towards the colorful glassy cups. Her palms had become numb. The cold tips of her fingers touched the mug of coffee which had become cold now. She could feel her heart beats and was afraid if she breathed, her heart would stop pumping.

The lead musician pointed to the drummer and the pianist and murmured: "1, 2, 3". While beating with his left foot, he glanced at the corner of the café.

Waiting was useless. He smiled and grabbed his instrument tightly with his sweaty hands., took a deep breath and held his instrument closer to his mouth. He was worried.

Suddenly, he saw the shadow of tall woman who was leaving the café in a hurry. The woman pulled away the heavy thick curtain in front of the entrance door and disappeared. The saxophone player thought to himself: "Who was that woman? Why didn't she stay longer?"

"THE SHAWL"

Ghambareh Gazan covered his dark face with the snowy-white Cashmere shawl. He had wrapped the shawl around his head so that only his two eyes were visible. His eyes, as blue as an ocean, were showing off. He knew that everyone could recognize those eyes very well. Sometimes he wishes nobody could.

When he was wandering the alleys and passages of the city, people would walk past him without paying any attention. But after noticing him, they would ask: 'Ghambareh Gazan, why have you wrapped the shawl around your head so tightly? Has anything happened?' He would reply with smiling eyes: 'No, I worked a bit longer yesterday in the boat. I caught a touch of the sun.' And as soon as he walked away from them, he would unwrap the shawl swiftly and curse himself: 'Stupid! Why do you cover your face when everyone can recognize you by your eyes, the way you walk and your body? Have you ever left this damn hot, sandy island for even a day?' But the following day, after having a glimpse at the Cashmere shawl which was whiter than snow, he would think: 'Today the foreigners might arrive and won't recognize me with my shawl.'

But he knew that those ugly, rich foreigners with their red ships a thousand times bigger than his worn-out wooden boat only visit once a year; when the gold fish lay eggs. Then they buy them so cheap and take the eggs to faraway lands to sell them far much, much more.

Is it our fault that gold fish have chosen this remote island? Ghambareh Gazan would tell lies to himself one after another. He knew that he was not the problem. The problem was the shawl. He couldn't stay away from it for a second. It was wrapped around his head, hands, neck; wherever he was and whatever he did. Sometimes he just didn't want anything else with or around his but that shawl. It had disordered his life. Sometimes he would wake up to check whether the shawl hadn't fallen off the bed.

He would always roll the shawl around his neck when working on the boat. Even though sometimes he felt stuffy, he was so careful not to drop it into the ocean. He was afraid the mermaids might get excited and wreck his boat to steal his shawl. He knew that they were the only ones who would appreciate its real beauty.

He remembered it was the first time in his life he had received a big parcel behind the door. He had become so excited that he ran upstairs and displayed the parcel to his landlord, his wife and chubby son who were stuffing their faces with fish omelet. While he was running around the room, he repeated: 'Look, what I've found at my doorstep. Look, what I've found at my doorstep. Look, what I've found at my doorstep.' And his landlord put the morsel he was going to bite down and said: 'Alright! Alright! Come and sit here to see what they have sent you.'

When he opened the parcel and got his hand on it he felt he had touched the softest and finest thing in the world and when he took it out he fell in love with its pure, immaculate color.

The landlord said: 'WOW! Such a nice gift! Now you go downstairs so we can have our breakfast.'

While he was going downstairs he had opened the shawl. A small piece of paper fell to the floor. He bent and picked it up. Looking at the note curiously, he read loudly: 'snowy-colored shawl for you, only you.'

He wore it around his neck for the first time and noticed the spark in his eyes immediately. He walked forward. His unruly blue eyes became calm. Even his eyes were enjoying it. It may have been the loneliness, the heat, both or none of them. It didn't matter to him anymore. The shawl was his, only his.

"00:00:00"

"**A**re you angry?" S asked to break the ongoing silence, in a voice he hoped sounded masterful.

Trying to stare less frequently at the clock in front of him, he moved his eyes to the man sitting opposite. 14 minutes and 34 seconds had passed and they had hardly exchanged any words.

Out of the corner of his eye, Mr S noticed a light flashing in the sky and reflecting on the polished multi-layered wooden table. He jerked as the thunder startled him. He moved on his chair to hide his fright. Then he put both his hands on the table and repeated: "Are you angry?"

In his expensive black suit, Mr F was sitting crossed-legged on a white leather sofa. He put his hands on his knees and he stared at the floor. He could have been meditating.

The picture was a blur to S. He felt imbalanced.

"It doesn't matter anymore. There isn't any time left. I don't know what I was thinking," said F worrying the sleeve button of his jacket. He kept silent for a second and then continued playing with his button faster and harder. He tried to pull it out, but it was tightly attached to his sleeve.

S grinned and appreciated the famous Italian tailor. All of a sudden, F stopped fiddling with the button, bent forward slightly, picked up the cushion he was leaning against, held it tight in his arms and said: "Yes, yes, I'm angry."

"Because you failed?" asked S.

F gave S a sharp look. Looking F in the face, S reminded him, "You know that you should talk. This is part of our agreement."

F took a deep breath and continued: "OK! Yes, I'm angry because I didn't foresee the situation… Because I took a wrong action and it changed everything."

"Life is unpredictable; so are people's reactions to change," said S. "Sometimes the decision you take can turn your world upside down."

"Yes, yes, and this is really scary."

Everything seemed vague to S. He had a quick look at the clock. 17 minutes and 58 seconds gone. Eighteen minutes and then there'd be ten minutes left to the end of the session, of which five would be spent on Mr F drinking chamomile tea, and him drinking strong coffee. He was expecting Ms H to enter the room in a minute, as he could hear her heels.

He could tell that Ms H was preparing the drinks since the rhythm of her heels was faster than usual. She had told Mr S that she never enjoyed making tea or coffee; it was not part her job after all. She just wanted to get it done with.

On the other hand, when she was filing, her heels would go slower and quieter. For her tidying up was like what a Friday evening cigar with a glass of scotch was for him – while his tall, thin apartment windows vibrated to the sound of Dvorak's violoncello concerto in B minor.

It had already started raining. The wind was shaking the branches of the hazelnut tree standing in front of the window. The twigs were rattling against it. It sounded like a drunkard was knocking on the door impatiently. This was how Mr S felt. The heels were getting closer and closer. After a few seconds, there was a knock at the door and little shadows appeared under it.

"Come on in," commanded Mr S. Mr F instantly put himself together.

"Don't worry, the tea is here," Mr S calmed him.

As she entered the room, Ms H was holding the tea tray in one hand and pulling down her skirt with the other hand. She bent and put the cup of tea in front of Mr F. She faked the most artificial smile that she could make and asked Mr F if he'd like some Swiss honey with his tea.

"No I like it without the honey" replied Mr F with a naughty smile.

S had a sip of his Turkish coffee, closed his eyes to savour the moment.

F started talking while he was eyeing up Ms H's legs: "That's weird." Ms H was already closing the door.

"What's weird?" asked Mr S.

"Women have either beauty or brains; one only."

S smiled and said: "There are ..."

"Really?" F said: 'If you know one, let me know'. I'm tired of talking with these dolls who when you tell them about the problems in Kashmir, they think you are talking about fabrics. I wish I could tell them what's wrong with Cashmere fabrics."

"Would you like to talk about the subject that you have already changed? Shall we stick to the point?"

F moved in his seat, stamped his feet, pulled himself up and said, "Till next session then."

With his cold and sweaty hands, he pressed Mr S's warm and wet hand and without waiting for him to utter a word, he walked briskly to the door and closed it behind himself very gently. It seemed like he had stolen something and did not want the noise of the door to wake anybody.

Mr S office was a place where everyone could speak frankly and honestly about their past and their deepest, darkest feelings without being judged. But why did people still manage to lie?

Without looking at the time, he reset the clock. He had not taken any notes today. He closed his thick, heavy diary and stared at the six digits. He pressed the reset button and the second hand started counting very fast. He stood up, walked to the other side of the desk and sat gently on the white sofa. Without paying any attention, he drank the rest of Mr F's tea, cleared his throat and looked at where he was sitting a few seconds ago. Then he shut his eyes and he pictured himself there.

He opened up, poured out his thoughts, feelings. He screamed, cried, laughed and then took a deep breath, lay on the sofa, and drew his legs up to his chest. After a while, he opened his eyes and got up gently and walked towards his desk and sat on his black leather seat.

He pressed the button and said Ms H, "Next patient, please."

Printed in the United States
By Bookmasters